Mystery of the Phony Murder

The Dallas O'Neil Mysteries

MYSTERY OF THE PHONY MURDER

by

JERRY B. JENKINS

MOODY PRESS

CHICAGO

© 1989 by
JERRY B. JENKINS

ISBN: 0-8024-8388-7

1 2 3 4 5 6 Printing/LC/Year 93 92 91 90 89

Printed in the United States of America

To Brett Swanger

Contents

1

The Code of Truth

First off, you need to know that I know better. I mean, I should know better. I've learned this lesson enough times. When my best friend, Jimmy Calabresi, first told me about it, I should have just reported it or made sure he did. But no, we wanted to be detectives. We wanted to check it out for ourselves.

To be totally honest, I didn't believe Jimmy at first anyway. He likes to pretend, to tell tall stories, to draw people in and then laugh at them when they believe him. That's what made it so hard for him to convince the rest of us in the Baker Street Sports Club when he finally got Star Diamond, the golden palomino he had always wanted.

Usually I could tell when Jimmy was lying—well, teasing. He never lied to get out of trouble or to get anyone else in trouble. His stories were always meant to be fun, and I guess they had always been harmless, except when he got someone's hopes up and then disappointed him.

But this time, I couldn't tell. I thought he was kidding, though he was trying to persuade me he was serious, but when you've been burned as many times as I have, you want to go into these things with your eyes wide open. That's why I probably made Jimmy mad with my silly grin and my tone of voice that said loudly, "It won't surprise me to find out you're putting me on."

How it happened was this:

It was a Friday night in November. I had just gotten home from a tough basketball game. Baker Street had lost by two on a last second shot. Jimmy had been our leading scorer for the first time ever, and I had had a bad game. I played OK on defense, but I scored only nine points, and the rest of the guys had to encourage me for once, instead of the other way around. Nobody wanted to go out afterward like we usually do, so we just rode home on our bikes and split up.

I wasn't in the house ten minutes before Jimmy called. I had already told my parents about the game and how I worried that we may never get out of second place with just twelve more games to play.

Mom told me the phone was for me. "It's Jimmy."

"Yo, Jim."

"Dallas, can you come over?"

It wasn't his typical way of asking, where he just wonders if I'm free. He sounded desperate. "I doubt it," I said. "What's up?"

"I can't tell you on the phone, but you have to come. I need you."

"Jimmy, I'm tired. If this is some kinda gag — "

"It's not. Now can you come or not?"

"I'll check, but I gotta tell ya, I wouldn't mind gettin' to bed."

"Check and see if you can come. It's important, but don't make such a big deal out of it that you have to answer questions later."

I asked my parents if I could go to Jimmy's if I promised to be home by ten-thirty. I reminded them it was not a school night.

"I don't mind you going," my dad said. "But I'd rather you not ride home on your bike that late. I don't want to have to come and get you, and I don't want the Calabresis to have to bring you home that late either. You'd better just go over tomorrow."

I told Jimmy.

"That may be too late," he said. "I'm making notes and trying to remember everything I need to tell you, but I want it to be fresh in my mind so I don't forget any of it. I won't be able to sleep anyway, so I'll be good for nothin' tomorrow. You gotta come tonight."

"I can't! Just tell me what's up."

"I told you, I can't tell you on the phone. Hey, how about if you come and stay over? Ask 'em that."

"Ask *your* mother first," I said. "No sense wastin' permission on this end if you can't get it on yours. Anyway, that'll be the first thing they ask me here."

"Hang on," Jimmy said, then came back on and said, "It's all right. Ask 'em, and I'll wait."

I asked.

"Is it all right with his mother?" Mom asked.

"Yup."

"You go straight over there and call us when you arrive."

I said I would. I threw a change of clothes in a bag and rode over. Even though it wasn't that late yet, it was still a little creepy riding in the country at night. When I got there I told Jimmy, "This better be good."

Jimmy dragged me up to his room. I have to admit, Jimmy has the best room of any of our friends. It's the highest room in the house, in what used to be the Calabresis' attic. It's not huge, but there's enough room for two beds. The ceiling slants to a point, and you get the feeling that you're upstairs in some cabin in the woods. His window looks out over Star Diamond's corral.

"Sit down," he said. "You're not gonna believe this."

Truer words were never spoken.

He told me he had beat his parents home from the game and that as he was walking by the phone in the living room—

11

"you know, that one on the lamp stand by the chair"—it rang. "It was like a half ring, sort of. In fact, by the time I got to it, I figured the line would be dead, because that little half ring happened just once and the thing was quiet for several seconds by the time I picked it up. I said hello, and I heard two voices. For some reason, they couldn't hear me."

"Maybe they were talking when you were."

"That's what I thought, but I said hello several more times and even talked louder, but they couldn't hear me at all."

"What were they saying?"

"That's just it. At first I had no idea. They were just talking about some business deal. I know I should have hung up, but I was curious. Fortunately, my mom keeps that tiny pad of paper under the phone and has a pen stuck to the back of the phone, so I wrote down some of it. Here's what I remember. It was an older guy talkin' to a younger guy.

"The older guy says something like, 'So, you're gonna do this? You're not gonna wimp out on me at the last minute, are ya?'

"The younger guy says, 'I hope not. I need the money.'

"The older guy says, 'That's not good enough, Calvin. I don't need hope; I need guarantees.'

"Calvin says, 'Duane, I've never done anything like this before. I can't guarantee anything.'

"Duane—the older guy—says, 'If you can't guarantee the job, you got no job, and I keep my ten grand.'

"Calvin says, 'No. I'll do it. As of right now, I'm plannin' on doin' it. I just hope I don't mess it up, that's all.'

"Duane says, 'That's a good thing to hope, Cal, because if you mess it up, you never hearda me, you got it?'

"'I know. It's just, you know, how do you make sure and get away clean?'

"'That's your problem, buddy boy. I'm countin' on ya. Run it down for me again how you're gonna do it.'

"So this younger guy, this Calvin, starts in about how he's gonna take this other guy for a ride and get him out in the country, then fake car trouble, and then 'off' him."

"*Off* him?"

"Yeah."

"What does that mean?"

"What do you *think* it means?"

"I have no idea, Jimmy. This is *your* story, not mine."

"This is no story. This is what I heard."

"Uh-huh. Just like on TV, Duane and Calvin are gonna 'off' some guy."

"That wasn't the only word they used for it."

"Oh, really? What else did they call it, whatever it is?"

"You know what it is just as well as I do, Dallas. It's murder."

I laughed. I couldn't help it. I didn't mean to. But I did. That made Jimmy really mad.

"You're the only person I told this to, Dallas, and now you think it's funny."

"I'm sorry," I said, still unable to fight a smile. "Tell me what else they called this, uh, murder."

Jimmy stood and went to the window, as if he was stalling for time. I knew he was either offended and was wondering if he should tell me anything more, or he was trying to really pull a funny one on me and was trying to think of a way to convince me it was true.

"Well," he said, turning back to me. "Once the older guy, Duane, referred to it as 'snuffing' the guy."

I burst out laughing. "Snuffing the guy! Ha! These guys are straight out of comic books, Jimmy! Tell me more!"

"All right, O'Neil, just forget it. You think I'm making this all up, so fine. Just never mind."

"No! Don't stop now! I love this! What else did they call it? Are they gonna take him for a ride? Are they gonna punch his lights out? Are they gonna plunk him?"

Jimmy pursed his lips, hating my reaction, but remember, I still didn't know for sure if it bugged him that I was onto his tall tale, or if he really had heard this and didn't know how to convince me. It did run through my mind that what he was telling me might actually have been said, but who knew whether it was real or if he was overhearing a radio station or pranksters or something?

"Well," he said reluctantly, "Calvin did say something about having the guy 'wasted.'"

"Oh, wow, they didn't leave anything out, did they?"

"Well," he said again, "they made some arrangement for the payoff."

"They did?" I was still fighting a smile. "You mean after the dastardly deed is done?"

"Yes, but if you're gonna make fun of me, I'm not gonna tell you any more."

"I don't mean to be making fun of you, Jimmy, but you know how you love to fool me. What if I buy this whole story and then you laugh your head off and say, 'I got you, Dallas, I got you real good!'?"

"That's what you're worried about?"

"Exactly. Why not?"

"'Cause I'm telling you the truth."

"How do I know that?"

"I'm your best friend, and I'm tellin' you, that's why."

"You've got me before doing that."

Jimmy sighed. "You think I made this whole thing up just for a little joke on you?"

I shrugged.

"Don't be ridiculous, Dal. It wouldn't be worth the effort. Anyway, it wouldn't be that funny."

"It would if I fell for it, as crazy as the story is."

Jimmy shook his head. "I give up," he said.

"You admit you're lying?"

"Nope."

"Then don't give up."

"You know, Dallas, in our family we have a code of truth."

"What's that?"

"We tell each other all kinds of stories, but if someone comes right out and asks us, 'Are you telling the truth?' we have to tell them the absolute truth. Not, 'Are you serious?' or, 'Are you kidding?' or, 'Are you lying?' The question is, 'Are you telling the truth?'"

"And it works?"

"'Course it works. We can't ever break the code. Otherwise we can't trust each other."

"So in other words, if I ask you that question, in those words, you have to tell me the absolute truth."

"Right."

"And if I find out you didn't?"

"You won't find that out. I would never violate the code."

"All right, then I want to know."

"Wanna know what?"

"If you're tellin' the truth."

"About what?"

"About this whole phone call deal—everything you've told me since I've been here."

"So ask me the question."

"I just did."

"No, you gotta ask it in just those words."

"You mean, 'Are you telling the truth?'"

"Right."

"OK, are you telling the truth?"

Jimmy looked me right in the eye. "Yes," he said, nodding.

I believed him, and it was right then that I should have told someone or insisted that he did. But instead I just asked him about the payoff arrangement.

2

The Call

Jimmy said that Duane, the older guy, told Calvin, "I'll bring an envelope with half of the ten G's and leave it for you in a hollowed out stump just in front of the shrubbery off the frontage road."

"Where's that?" Calvin asked.

"Just before the Toboggan Road exit near Baker Street."

"How far is that from Olive, where that mall is with the grocery store?"

"Not far, not far. You know the place."

"Yeah. Hey, Duane?"

"Yeah."

"What's gonna keep me from stiffin' you and makin' off with half the dough?"

"What're you, stupid?"

"What do you mean?"

"You think *I'm* stupid, Calvin?"

"Well, I guess if you give me half of ten grand before I do the job, yeah, you're stupid."

"The older guy swears," Jimmy told me, "and then he explains to Calvin how he's giving him half the money, literally."

"What did he mean by that?" I asked.

"He said he was giving him half of each five hundred dollar bill."

"Half of each?"

"Yup. He told Calvin he was going to tear twenty-five hundred dollar bills in two and leave the left halves in an envelope in the tree stump."

"What's the point of that?"

"That's what Calvin asked, and Duane started yelling at him about how stupid he was and how scared Duane was that he had ever asked the idiot to become involved at all."

"Did he ever explain it?" I asked.

"I'm getting to that. He said that half a bill was worthless, so that what he kept and what he gave Calvin was worthless until they were put back together."

I raised my eyebrows. "So Duane proves he's got the money by giving Calvin half of each bill. When does Calvin get the other halves?"

"When the murder is committed."

"How does he know it was done?"

"Calvin has to prove it."

"How's he supposed to do that?"

"I don't even want to think about it."

"Well, what did this Duane say? Surely he's not going to take Calvin's word for it."

"He just said he needed solid proof."

"Yuck."

When the phone rang, we both jumped. Jimmy ran for the door, hoping to beat his parents to the phone. When he swung the door open we heard Mr. Calabresi.

"Jimmy! Tell Dallas his mother's on the phone!"

She was mad. "You promised to call as soon as you got there," she said. "We were worried sick."

"Why didn't you just call?"

"I *did*! But *you* were supposed to call *us*!"

"Sorry, Mom." I was tempted to tell her why I forgot all about it.

"Don't let it happen again, or you won't be allowed to go to Jimmy's again."

I told her I understood and apologized again. She hung up before I did and suddenly my heart went cold. Jimmy had not been kidding. I heard the voices.

"I'm not going to tell you when I'm leaving it," a man said. "But you can pick it up at five in the morning."

"OK," the other voice said. The voice sounded younger. That had to be Calvin.

When I got back upstairs, my face must have been white. Jimmy believed me immediately. "What are we gonna do?" he said.

"Are you kidding?" I said.

"Are you thinking what I'm thinking?"

I nodded.

"On our bikes?"

I shook my head. "You have to get up early to muck out Star Diamond's stall anyway, right?"

"Yeah."

"So no one will think twice about your taking him for an early morning ride."

"Yeah, but what if we find the money and leave horse tracks?"

"We won't get that close with the horse, Jimmy. Now let's get to sleep so we can get up early."

"How early?"

"Four?"

Jimmy set his alarm clock, but we hardly slept a wink. I finally dropped off at about three-thirty, so when that alarm rang at four, it startled me. We dressed and moved around the bedroom and bathroom like zombies, not even speaking to each other.

I watched as Jimmy mucked out the big palomino's stall. It was earlier than the stallion was used to, and he stamped and snorted in confusion, but Jimmy soothed him.

19

"I'm gettin' a bad feeling about this, Dallas," Jimmy said, hesitating near the saddle that straddled the top of the stable door.

"It'll be fun," I said, trying to convince myself as much as him. "There's no danger. We can tie the horse to a tree off the road a ways, and then walk the last hundred yards or so. If the money can be found by five, it must be there by now."

"It'll be dark. How will we see anything?"

"I'd rather have that problem than worry that someone was going to see us." I looked at my watch. "We gotta go."

He lifted the saddle and motioned toward the blanket with his head. I slung the blanket over the horse's back, and Jimmy strapped on the saddle. The horse stutter-stepped in his stall in anticipation of being ridden. Jimmy put the bit, bridle, and reins on him, backed him out of the stall, led him out of the stable, and hopped up. Jimmy pulled his foot out of the stirrup so I could get mine in, then reached down to help me up. When I was behind him I let him have the stirrup back, and we started off.

Jimmy and I looked at our watches at the same time, and he gently tapped Star Diamond's underbelly with the insides of his feet, made a noise with his mouth, and urged the big horse to go faster. When we got to the frontage road, I leaned up to Jimmy's ear. "Let's tie him up over there," I said, pointing to a grove of trees back off the road about fifty feet. There's lots of underbrush around there.

"Anywhere he can graze?"

"I think so. Let's check."

Jimmy ambled the horse down into a clearing where we couldn't be seen from the road. There was enough moonlight to see a good spot to tie him where he could nibble at the grass and weeds. Jimmy patted the horse's neck, and we headed out to where we thought the stump was that Duane had referred to. We were surprised to see three stumps in the moonlight.

"Which one's the one?" Jimmy whispered.

I shrugged. "Only one way to find out."

"Be careful," he said.

"What do you mean, be careful? You're comin' with me. You be careful too."

We crept out from the trees more than a hundred yards from Star Diamond and still out of sight from the frontage road. Every time we heard a car hiss by on the pavement we stopped and prepared to dive for cover, in case it turned in. Finally we reached a big tree that hid us from the road and the stumps. We peeked out at them.

"You take the one on the left," I said. "I'll check the middle and the one on the right."

"What am I looking for?" Jimmy asked.

"An envelope, of course. What did you think?"

He shrugged. "How should I know? I have no idea what to do if I find an envelope either."

"Just look in it. See if it's got the twenty halves of five hundred dollar bills."

"What if it does?"

"Then just tell me."

"Where's it supposed to be hidden?"

"In a hollow spot, I s'pose. Now let's go!"

I scampered out to the middle stump, sensing and hearing Jimmy behind me. The stump was big but seemed fresh. There was no hole, no rot, not soft spot, nothing left from where someone might have tried to burn or destroy the stump. I felt all around it. Nothing. Jimmy had already dashed back to behind our tree.

I felt around the smaller stump on the right. There were two holes in it. One felt as if someone had drilled it cleanly through the top. The other felt soft and crumbly, like rotted wood from years of decay. There was nothing in either of the holes. I hurried back to Jimmy.

His back was pressed up against the tree, and he was panting. "Did you run?" I asked.

He shook his head.

"Well?" I pressed.

He shook his head again.

"Nothing?"

This time he nodded.

I was confused. "Well," I said, "what are you saying? Yes, you didn't find anything, or no, you didn't find nothing, you found something?"

He nodded again.

"You're gonna hafta tell me, Jim," I said. "You've lost me."

He nodded vigorously and pointed toward his stump. "Over there," he managed. "There's an envelope in that stump."

"Did you check it?" I asked. "Anything in it?"

He shook his head again. I didn't know whether he hadn't checked it, or if he had and found nothing in it. He wasn't saying much, so I knew I would have to find out for myself. I stepped out toward the stump just as Jimmy whispered. "Dallas!" he rasped. "Take cover."

"Car?" I said, freezing.

"No! Bike!"

I dove for cover.

3

Calvin

I slid back behind a tree and saw a young man, maybe in his late twenties, ride up on a ten-speed bike. He slowed as he moved off the pavement and onto the grass, and he rode slowly near the three tree stumps, looking closely at each one. I held my breath. Then he rode off.

When I was certain he was out of earshot, I rasped, "I would have bet my life he was the pick-up man."

"Me too," Jimmy said. "That had to be Calvin. But why didn't he stop? You think he saw us?"

"I hope not. But he might just have been scouting the area to be sure no one was around."

"Where are you going, Dallas?!"

"Shh! I'm gonna see if that envelope is what we think it is."

I tiptoed out to the stump and pulled the envelope out to where I could see it in the faint early morning light. It was sealed, but I was shocked when I turned it over and noticed the oval-shaped hole cut into the front of it. The envelope was one of those that banks provide for people who want to give cash gifts. The only time I had seen them before was when my grandparents sent me a crisp, new ten dollar bill in one for my birthday.

I could tell from the thickness that this one had a stack of bills in it, but all I could see from the hole in the front was that they had all been cut in half. I held the envelope out into the light and saw half a picture and half a name, the letters M-C-K-I. So the picture was of President McKinley. I wondered if these were five hundred dollar bills. I was tempted to open the envelope, but it wasn't mine, and it was sealed. I wondered if I could bend them enough to pull them out through the oval cut-out in the front, just to see if I was right.

I felt terribly conspicuous standing there in the clearing near the stump, so I slowly walked toward the tree again. Just as I reached it, Jimmy made a desperate noise from where he hid. "Psst!"

I jerked to look at him, and he was signaling frantically for me to hide. I slipped behind the tree and held my breath. Here came the bicyclist again, only this time he dismounted and felt around the stumps just like we had. So this was our man, this was Calvin, and he was looking for the first half, literally, of his payoff.

And there I stood with it. What if he had seen it when he rode by the first time and just circled back to get it when he was sure no one was around? I could have kicked myself. *He* sure did some kicking. When he discovered nothing in any of the stumps, he kicked one of them, then kicked dirt and grass and swore at himself. "You're a fool, Calvin," he raged, "thinkin' you're gonna get rich off some scheme like this!"

He hurried back to his bike, but instead of riding away he dropped it and ran back to the stumps, searching them more carefully this time, reaching deep into the holes and scraping dead wood out. He walked slowly to his bike and rode away.

"What do I do now?" I asked Jimmy.

"Oh, now I'm the expert, huh?" he said. "This whole caper is your idea, and now you're left holding the bag and you're askin' me for advice. Great!"

"Well, I don't know what to do."

"Start by puttin' that money back where it belongs, Dallas. This guy wants it so bad he'll probably think twice and come back for one more look."

"How can I make it look like it was there all along and he just missed it?"

"Don't ask me! You're the detective."

I strolled back out to the stump and looked for a way to put the envelope back in such a way that Calvin, if that's who was looking for it, would think he had overlooked it. I tried pushing it down deep into the decayed hole, but it was too obvious that I had just done it.

Then I noticed a split in the outside of the trunk on the side away from his line of vision. Would it be possible for him to think he had overlooked that, if I could slide it in far enough? The only problem was that if he told Duane where he found it, and Duane remembered having put it in the hole, they would both know someone had been tampering with it and at least knew about the money.

I didn't have any choice. I set the end of the envelope on the edge of the split and tapped it gently. It slid in deep, just a corner of the envelope sticking out. Then I heard the bike again and dashed for the tree.

It was just as Jimmy predicted. It looked as if Calvin simply wasn't ready to give up looking for half his money. Or maybe he had called Duane in a rage, and Duane had insisted that he had left the money there.

Calvin was angry and in a hurry. He slid right up to the stumps, dropped the bike, and rummaged around the stumps. It was so strange to know what he was looking for, know right where it was, and yet be unable to help him find it.

Most amazing was when he didn't find it where I had left it! I blinked and stared when he pulled the envelope up out of the decaying hole through the top. I almost gasped and had to keep from getting into a better position to see. I waited until he tore the envelope open, dropped it, counted the halves of five hundred dollar bills, and stuffed them in his pocket.

He looked relieved and a lot happier when he jumped aboard his bike and raced off. We waited longer this time to be sure he didn't come back and that no one else was around. Finally we walked out into the clearing. I picked up the empty envelope and put it in my pocket.

"I don't believe what I just saw," Jimmy said. "I know you put that envelope in the split in the side of the trunk. He didn't even look or feel there, but he came up with it anyway."

"I know," I said.

"How do you figure it?"

"I don't know. It must be that the hole had almost been eaten through to the split. When I tapped the envelope, it must have broken through and could then be reached from the top."

"Do you think he'll be suspicious, Dal? I mean, how's he gonna explain that he missed it the first and second times he looked and found it the third?"

I shrugged. How did I know?

"I hate to admit it," I said, "but now I wish we hadn't brought the horse."

"Why? Calvin went the other way both times. He couldn't have seen Star Diamond."

"I know he didn't see him, but I'd like to find out where Calvin is going, and we can hardly follow him on a horse without being noticed."

"I think we can," Jimmy said. "We can at least try. But are you sure you want to follow a guy who's plannin' on killin' somebody?"

"Not really. But who knows if we'll ever get the chance to hear them on the phone again. We don't know where the crime is supposed to happen or anything. I didn't even get a good enough look at Calvin to be able to identify him."

We ran to the horse. "We've got to go north," Jimmy said.

We mounted quickly and Star Diamond galloped off. We quickly emerged from the trees and caught sight of Calvin pedaling up the frontage road.

"How far away can he hear the horseshoes?" I asked.

"I'll get back onto soft ground when we get closer."

Calvin never once turned around while we followed him. When he turned right, Jimmy ducked his horse down into the trees and rode to the trees at the side of the road ahead of Calvin. We dismounted quickly and crept to the edge of the trees. By now it was dawn, light enough to get a good look at him.

He was smiling as he pedaled by. He was wearing a baseball cap with black hair curling out from beneath it. He had dark eyes and a long nose. I was struck by how white and even his teeth were. I didn't know what a murderer should look like. He looked kind of young and innocent and almost friendly.

"I hope he turns left," I said.

"Why?"

I nodded into the distance. If Calvin went left, we could watch him for a long time from right where we were. In fact, if we got up in a tree, we could watch him for almost a mile. There were just a few lone trees here and there. We looked at each other and smiled when Calvin turned left.

I helped Jimmy get started up a tree, and then he reached down and helped me up. We climbed almost to the top of a thirty- or forty-foot pine. With both of us that high the skinny treetop began to sway, and we both whooped and backed down a couple of feet.

"Oh, no," Jimmy said, as I kept my eyes glued on Calvin, riding his bike in the distance.

"What?" I said without turning.

"Star Diamond," he said softly.

I turned and looked. The horse had worked free of the tree where Jimmy had loosely tied him. He was moving about, lazily grazing. "What're you going to do?" I asked.

"I'd better go down," he said. "If something spooks him and he breaks into a trot, we'll never catch him."

"Whatever," I said, "but I want to stay up here and see which way Calvin goes."

When I turned to watch him again, he was out of sight. I panicked, but soon he appeared from the other side of a homestead, and then he turned in at the next place. Was it possible? Was he the bachelor who had moved into the old Blakely place? We had heard someone finally bought the place, which had stood empty for years. Rumors said the buyer was a young man who worked in Park City and didn't even plan to farm the ground or pay to have someone else do it.

I wanted to call down to Jimmy, but I didn't want to startle the horse. I looked down. Jimmy was slowly coming up to Star Diamond and talking softly to him. Once he had the reins, I said, "We can ride by Calvin's place, Jim. Guess where he pulled in?"

"The Blakely's?" he asked.

"Yup."

Getting down was a lot easier than getting up.

"You really want to ride by there?"

"Don't you?"

"I don't think I want him to have a look at us."

"Well, maybe we can get a look at something that will give us some more clues without him seeing us."

"Sounds too risky."

"Riskier than what we've done already? Let's go!"

"Dallas, slow down. You're gonna get us into big trouble. Let's at least go home and get our bikes. That'll make it a lot easier, and we won't stick out so much."

"True," I said. "Now that we know where he lives, we don't have to keep him in sight all the time."

We mounted the horse.

"Dallas?"

"Yeah."

"Have you prayed about this yet?"

"Why?"

"'Cause it seems like the type of a thing you would usually pray about, and you haven't said anything about it."

I was embarrassed. "I prayed when Calvin showed up at the stumps and I had his cash envelope."

"I'll bet you did," Jimmy said. "But seriously—"

"I know," I said. "I prayed a little about it when I couldn't sleep last night."

"Me too," he said. "And I don't know what God is gonna tell us to do, but I sure want Him to know that I have no great ideas."

"I don't have any either," I said. "But I sure want to find out if Calvin actually lives where we think he lives."

4

The Discovery

When we got back to Jimmy's the rest of his family was up and getting ready for breakfast. Jimmy put the horse in the corral, and we decided to eat so we wouldn't look too suspicious.

"Where have you boys been?" Mrs. Calabresi asked.

"We took Star Diamond up to the frontage road and around there."

"Good."

Mr. Calabresi came into the kitchen. "Who was that on the phone earlier?" he said.

"Oh, that was the strangest thing," his wife said, and I was paralyzed. I glanced at Jimmy who was looking at me. "It was a wrong number or something. I mean, I could hear two men talking and yet they couldn't hear me."

"Were they trying to reach us?"

"I don't think so. Somehow their call made our phone ring, but what they said didn't have anything to do with us."

I wanted to ask what they said so badly that I almost did. But Mr. Calabresi was curious too, and he asked.

"Well, it was something about whether one of them got what he was looking for and did anybody see him. I couldn't follow it too well. The one said there had been no problem and that no one saw him, and then the other said something about whether everything was set for next Friday night."

"Hm," Jimmy's dad said. "Wonder what's happening then?"

"They didn't say. I kept trying to cut in and make myself heard, but they couldn't hear me. As soon as they'd set their time and place, I hung up."

I was certain she would say where and when, and if she didn't, I just knew Mr. Calabresi would ask. But he didn't. And she didn't say. I was dying.

She continued. "I called the phone company, not thinking how early in the morning it was. All I got was a recording that told me to call after eight on regular business days. I want to see how that happens and whether there's anything we can do about it. I don't want to hear other people's calls, and I'm sure those gentlemen would be upset if they knew someone could hear them."

Would they ever!

"Ah, I wouldn't worry about it unless it happened a lot," Mr. Calabresi said. "Probably just some little equipment or wiring foul-up."

I thought of Basil, a guy at our church who works at the phone company. I would ask him. But for right now, I wanted to ask Mrs. Calabresi exactly where and when they would be and do what they were going to do Friday night. How could I get it out of her? How could I ask without looking suspicious or being too obvious?

Fortunately, she came back to it. "Whatever one of them is doing Friday at nine sure has him nervous. I guess he's trying to impress someone he's never met and he's taking him somewhere. He's going to pick him up behind the grocery store. I guess the guy manages the store."

She said it with such little interest that I could tell she had no idea what was happening. No one else at the table responded, and I'm sure they all forgot about it. Yet Jimmy and I had learned a lot of valuable information. We knew who the target victim was, where he worked, where he would be picked up, and when. That wouldn't do us much good unless we knew where they were going. No way we could keep up with a car on our bikes—or even on horseback—and I didn't think Jimmy would take Star Diamond into the alley behind the grocery store anyway.

After breakfast we hurried up to his room. "Somehow," I said, "you've got to be the one who answers the phone around here as often as possible. It sounds like every call this guy gets or makes somehow makes your phone ring. Your parents are gonna get real tired of it and have somebody fix it. Then we won't have any source of information."

"Except that we know where Calvin lives and when and where a lot of this is supposed to take place."

"That doesn't give us much, Jim. We need to know more."

"Dallas," Jimmy said slowly, "what are we gonna do about this?"

"What do you mean?"

"Just what I said. Surely we're not gonna just stand by and watch a murder take place."

"No, of course not."

"Well, what are we gonna do about it?"

I hadn't really thought that one through. "We'll, uh, stop it."

"Stop it?"

"Yeah."

"How?"

"We'll, uh, surprise Calvin and, uh, give the victim time to get away."

"And what about us?"

"Us, too."

"Us, too, what?"

"Will get away."

"And then we what? Tell the police?"

"Yeah."

"And it's our word against Calvin's?"

I shrugged.

"Dallas, I got to tell ya, you're haywire on this one."

I knew he was right, but I wasn't about to admit it. "What do you mean? Why?"

"You know as well as I do that we can't go doing all this stuff by ourselves. We've got to go to the police. We could go to them now. We know enough to give them a good start."

"Are you kidding? You think they'd believe a couple of kids? They'd have to check out our story, just to be sure."

"So let 'em check it. They'd find out we're tellin' the truth."

"Yeah, and then we'd be told to stay out of it. No way."

"I don't mind stayin' out of it. We're gettin' in over our heads."

"Oh, Jim, you gotta be kiddin'. I haven't had this much fun in a long time."

"Yeah, you're gonna fun us right into the grave. We better set some limit we won't go past."

"Like what?"

"Like we won't let the grocery store manager get into Calvin's car. If we do, we have to take responsibility for what happens to him, and you know what that will be."

I shrugged. "Maybe," I said.

Jimmy's mother called up the stairs. "We're going into town! You boys want to come?"

"No thanks, Mom. We're gonna stay around here for a while and then maybe ride bikes."

"OK. Don't go too far! We'll be back by five."

"Five! Where are you going?"

"The hardware store and the mall. We're going to take our time."

I couldn't believe our luck. "We can catch any phone calls, if they're still coming here," I said.

"Yeah, but who's going to scout Calvin's house?"

I thought a minute. "Do you mind if I do?" I asked.

"No, I'll wait by the phone," Jimmy said. "Why?"

"I've got a bunch of errands to run. I want to talk to somebody at the bank. I want to talk to Basil, our friend from church. I might even want to talk to the manager of the grocery store."

"Really?"

I nodded.

"What would you tell him?"

"I'd play it by ear."

Jimmy shrugged. "Whatever. You gonna cruise Calvin's, too?"

"Yup."

"Don't be gone long."

"I won't. Take good notes, just in case."

"Don't worry."

I rode as fast as I could to Basil's house. He seemed glad to see me, but he was busy in his garden. "Can I ask you a question?"

"You just did, partner," he said, smiling. "Try another."

"When you can hear someone else on your phone, what's the problem?"

Basil is a funny guy, and I could tell from the look in his eyes that he was going to tease me some more. "There's no problem," he said. "In fact, that's good. That's what phones are made for, ya know. So you can hear other people. It's handy that way, especially if they can hear you too."

I laughed. "That's just it. They can't hear me."

"But you can hear them?" He was serious now.

I nodded.

"Does the phone ring?"

"Yup."

"Cross talk," he said.

"What?"

"Cross talk. It usually happens when a new line has been installed. It can be fixed in a few seconds down at the office. Need to report some?"

"Hm?"

"Need to report some cross talk?"

"Oh, uh, no. Nah, not yet."

Basil straightened up and leaned on his rake, smiling. "You like what you're hearin', huh?"

"What?"

"Just kiddin', Dallas," he said. "I was just wonderin' if you were havin' some cross talk on your phone and you wanted to listen in a little longer before you have us do somethin' about it."

"We're not having any cross talk on our phone," I said. "A friend of mine is. I'll tell him what you said."

On my way to the grocery store on Olive Street I stopped at the bank where I first thought I would ask my question at the drive-up window. Then I thought better of it. I felt funny standing there in line with the cars, so I parked my bike and went in. I told one of the tellers I had a question about money, and when I told her it was about who was on what bill, she said, "Currency questions are handled in New Accounts."

In New Accounts a woman shocked me when I asked her what bill has President McKinley on it. "Well, now President McKinley's portrait appears on several pieces of currency. He's on a five thousand dollar U.S. savings bond and the five hundred million dollar treasury note. He's also — "

"Five hundred *million*?" I interrupted. "McKinley's on a five hundred million dollar bill? I didn't even know there was such a thing!"

"Yes, there is, and McKinley is also — "

"I can hardly believe it. Do those bonds and notes look just like dollar bills? Same size?"

"Not exactly the same size, no. But I've been trying to tell you that McKinley is also on the five hundred dollar bill, and that looks just like most other bills."

I nodded. That's just what I wanted to hear. I was pretty sure what I saw was the five hundred dollar bills. But I wanted to be really sure. "Would you be able to show me a five hundred dollar bill?" I said.

"We might have one around," she said. "But you know they're no longer in circulation."

"They're what?"

"No longer in circulation. They aren't made anymore, and as they come in to the federal reserve bank, they are taken out of circulation."

"What about people who still have some?"

"Well, it depends on where they got them. They were discontinued more than twenty years ago, so the serial numbers would be checked against known stolen currency, and if everything was in order, they would be honored."

"But if they were stolen?"

"They'd be easily traced."

5

Meeting the Target

I hardly knew what to say to the lady in New Accounts at the bank. I knew what I was asking her had nothing to do with opening a new account, so she was being kind in just taking the time to talk to me.

"Um, how does somebody know if the five hundred dollar bill he has, if he had one, I mean, is stolen?"

"You mean whether it has been laundered?"

"You mean run through the washing machine?" I said. I'd never heard of laundering money.

She smiled but didn't laugh. "No, you see, when people steal money, they try to pass it off by moving it through someone else's hands or accounts. For instance, if someone robbed a bank and took, say, several thousand dollars, they would want to launder it so it couldn't be traced to them. If they just went around and started spending it, someone could check the serial numbers and, if they matched those of the stolen money, trace it to the robbers."

I nodded. "So, how do they keep that from happening?"

"By laundering it. They run it through a bank account or spend it somewhere where no one will be suspicious. If they can somehow get it into their account without anyone realizing it has been stolen, they can then withdraw it by check or as different currency. Then no one will find out."

"Hm," I said. "I guess I don't really understand, but thanks for explaining it to me."

"Let me try again," she said. "I can tell you're just interested and you're not the type of a boy who wants to rob banks."

I laughed and nodded. "That's for sure."

"Well, for instance, one night last year, two stores in that little mall on Olive Street were burglarized the same night. It was a very risky type of a burglary because both stores had their safes broken into, yet the thief was never caught."

"What was so risky about it?"

"The alarm went off in the jewelry store when the safe was cracked. By the time the police got there, which wasn't long, the grocery store had been burglarized too. The alarm in its safe room went off while the police were in the jewelry store."

"Wow, that is risky. Why would somebody do that?"

"Nobody knows. I guess whoever did it figured all the attention would be on the jewelry store and that no one would expect the burglar to be a few hundred feet away pulling another job at the same time."

"So, did they catch the guy? Somebody must have seen the getaway car."

"No, that was what was so strange about it. The alarm was sounded by the grocery store manager, Frank Tresh. He said he was driving by when he saw all the police cars and lights and stopped in to make sure everything was all right at the store. When he got to the stock room, he saw the safe door was open and the cash was gone. Most of the store's money was usually deposited in the bank at closing, but there were several thousand there that they use to stock the cash drawers at all the registers."

"How do you know all this?" I asked.

"It happened on the same night we were robbed," she said. "Well, not robbed, but burglarized."

"What's the difference?"

"I'm not entirely sure, but I recall someone correcting me when I said we had been robbed. Something about a robbery having to do with some person being held up, while burglary is just stuff being stolen when nobody is around. Something like that."

"What did the bank lose?"

"Well, it's interesting that you should ask, because we lost a bag of five hundred dollar bills. There was a canvas bag with twenty-five stacks of one hundred bills each."

"And those were all five hundreds?" I said.

She nodded and slid a calculator across her desk to me. "Can you tell me how much that was?"

I punched in a hundred times twenty-five times five hundred. "One million two hundred and fifty thousand dollars?"

She nodded. "Very good. But for as good as the safe cracker was—and he was very good—he stole money that was just passing through here."

"Passing through?"

"It was a shipment of old out-of-circulation five hundreds that had been collected at a bank in the city and were simply left here on their way to the federal reserve bank in Washington. No one could have known about them, and if they had known about them, they would have known the currency was worthless. The numbers have all been recorded, and unless the money is laundered in some very unusual way, it won't be honored anywhere. That's why it was left out in the safe. It wasn't secured like most of our money. It was simply left on a table just inside the walk-in safe. Once the door was opened, the burglar probably just looked inside the bag and thought he'd made a killing. He didn't even try to get anything more."

"So if whoever has that money tries to spend it . . ?"

"It won't work. Private individuals may accept it as a payment of a debt, but when someone gets around to trying to spend it or deposit it or get it changed into smaller bills, no one will accept it, and certainly a bank won't. And should the teller, or whoever, have the presence of mind to check the serial numbers against the list of known stolen currency, the bearer will have some important questions to answer."

"The bearer?"

"The person with the money. He or she will have to be able to prove he got the money from somewhere other than our safe. Then the trail toward the burglar will begin."

I called Jimmy from the pay phone outside our library. "I'm gonna be a while longer," I said. "Any calls?"

"Yes," he said. "I heard them again. One of them mentioned the target's name, and—"

"Jimmy, let's not talk about this on the phone. I just wanted to tell you that I'm gonna be at the library for a while. I'm trying to check on something I just heard. Very interesting."

"What?"

"I'll tell you when I get back. I still have to go to the store and to the farm. You know."

"Yeah. Hurry. Maybe after you go to the store you can come and baby-sit and I'll go to the farm. You know."

"Yeah, that sounds like a good idea," I said. "I'll see you when I get back from the store."

In the library I went to the microfiche machine and looked up the front pages of the local newspaper for more than a year and a half before, where I finally found the stories of the burglaries of the jewelry store, the grocery store, and the bank. What I found very interesting was that, for a week or so, suspicion had centered on Frank Tresh.

The police couldn't figure why the alarm at the grocery store had not gone off while the burglar was there. Tresh was questioned for days and was even charged with the crime, but his lawyer argued that the only evidence was his fingerprints on the safe and in the stock room, where they would naturally be because of his job. His fingerprints were not found in the jewelry store or the bank, and he was never connected with anyone who might have taken the money. He was cleared, and

44

everyone assumed he was innocent. A few weeks later his friends threw a big party for him and presented him with a plaque for his bravery and for alerting the police so quickly.

After that his name disappeared from the news, except for about every other month after that when he was honored by some civic or business group as an outstanding businessman and once when his employees surprised him by naming him employee of the month.

I felt bad that this poor, innocent guy who just happened along at the right—or wrong—time had suffered so much. He had done the only thing he knew to do. The stock room and the safe had been broken into, so he pulled the alarm. How should he know why it hadn't gone off while the burglar was in there? Certainly the burglar had hit the grocery store before the jewelry store. Frank Tresh is just lucky he didn't walk in on the burglar while he was cracking open the safe.

I wanted to meet this guy.

I asked for him at the grocery store and was told that he was in the back where the produce department boys were receiving a shipment. I hung around back there and caught glimpses of him every time the double swinging doors swung open and shut. I recognized him from his picture on a poster at the front of the store that told who the manager-on-duty was. He was tall and thin with light brown hair, a flimsy mustache, and glasses. I guessed him to be in his mid-thirties.

As I watched, a little girl came hurrying up the aisle pushing another little girl in a wheelchair. She burst through the doors, squealing, "Daddy! Daddy!"

He scooped her up and bent down to kiss the younger one in the chair, then brought them out to meet his wife. He smiled and kissed her, and she scolded her daughter for getting away from her. He seemed happy to see her and certainly didn't appear to be thinking about the trouble in his store from more than a year ago.

I almost didn't want to bring it up. But after he said something to his wife about when he would be home for dinner and she took the girls out to the car, I asked if I could talk to him. He smiled and asked if I was looking for something.

"Just you," I said.

He motioned for me to follow him to his cramped little office in the back. "I'm expecting a salesman in a few minutes," he said, "but until then, I'm yours."

I jumped right in. "In the library I read the microfiche clips about the burglary in your store last year." His smile froze, and he nodded. "I was wondering if you had enough information about whoever did it or how it was done or anything to be a threat to the burglar."

He leaned back in his chair and raised his eyebrows. "An amateur detective, are you?"

I smiled and nodded. "I guess."

"Well, I'll tell ya, I almost wish I was a threat to him or her or them or whoever did it. I think if they were worried about me, I'd know about it by now. Don't you?"

That was a thought. Why did they wait so long to worry about him? I sensed it was too early to tell him what I knew. "So you didn't just recently go to the police with any new information? There's nothing new on the case?"

"No, I didn't, and there's nothing new on it that I know of. How about you?"

"Me?"

"Yeah. Anything new you've turned up, or did you just start getting into this when you read it in the library?"

"Sort of."

He smiled, and his phone rang. "OK, thanks," he said into the receiver. He put his hand over the mouthpiece. "My appointment is here, son. Sorry. Anything else I can do for you?"

"No, thanks. I might like to talk to you about it again sometime though, if that'd be all right."

"Well, it wasn't a very happy time for me," he said. "But, yeah, sure, anytime."

I could tell by the look on his face and the tone of his voice that he didn't expect to ever see or hear from me again. To him

I was just a kid with a curiosity. But there was one thing I knew for sure. If he didn't see or hear from me again before the next Friday night, he might be a dead man.

6

Getting Too Close for Comfort

I wanted to ride out and stake out Calvin's place, but I had promised Jimmy, in our cryptic phone conversation, that I would "baby-sit" and he could do that. Anyway, I was dying to hear what he had heard on the phone.

"Before I tell you everything I learned," I said, "you gotta tell me what they said."

"It was real strange," he said, "but I think I know why they want to kill Frank Tresh."

"Why? Does he know more than he's letting on? Is he going to the police?"

Jimmy shrugged. "I'm not sure," he said, "but I know he wants his money. His share."

"His share?" I was stunned. "He was in on it?"

"That's my guess," Jimmy said. "Duane was saying to Calvin something like, 'I'm not gonna let this guy blackmail me the rest of my life. I gave him twenty grand, which is more than I got from his part of the plan.'

"Calvin says, 'Duane, think about it. Call his bluff. If he goes to the police after all this time, it'll blow his own cover. How will he explain after over a year of insisting on his innocence that now he knows enough to get somebody busted for three jobs in the same night?'

"Duane says, 'I don't care. He says he's gonna go to 'em; I gotta believe him. And I can't let that happen.'

"Calvin says something about looking for another angle, another way to get at him, 'like through his family.'

"Duane says, 'Are you kiddin'? That's a federal offense, and anybody who knows me knows I ain't gonna waste no kid or wife.'

"Calvin says, 'Well, what do you think we're talkin' about here—somethin' that *isn't* a federal offense?'

"'I know,' Duane says, 'but it's quick and clean, and it's traditional. Anyway, he's got it coming. I upheld my part of the deal, he did his job, and he got paid. He's not gonna bleed me dry the rest of his life, which I hope ain't gonna be that long, if you know what I mean.'

"There was silence on the phone for a while after that," Jimmy said, "and I got worried that I had lost the connection, but it was just Calvin thinking. Duane got nervous too. He says, 'Calvin, we're a little late for you to be gettin' cold feet, OK? Don't make me stiff you too.'

"'Stiff me?' Calvin says. 'What do you mean, stiff me? I'm supposed to take that literally?'

"Duane says, 'Don't get squirrely on me, Cal. I'm just talkin' generalities here. I mean you don't do your job, you don't get the other half of the package. Know what I mean?'

"Calvin says, 'It seems to me you've got a worthless half of a package without me, Duane.'

"And now Duane gets mad. He starts breathing hard and sounding real tough. 'You know something, Calvin,' he says, 'you're a two-bit local punk. I eat guys like you for breakfast. You stiff me on ten grand, and what have you got? You've got nothin' but a boatload of trouble for the rest of your life. You got no money, but you got a number on your head. You'll have to look over your shoulder everywhere you go.'

50

"'You threatening me?' Calvin wants to know.

"'Stinkin' right I am,' Duane says, 'and it'll be more than a threat if you don't do what you said you'd do.'

"'Yeah,' Calvin says, 'but you won't do it yourself, will you? You'll hire local muscle.'

"'That's right,' Duane says, 'but I won't make the mistake of payin' a local punk big city dollars, the same kind of numbers I pay for a professional who knows better than to back out of a good deal.'

"'Oh, I'm not backing out, Duane,' Calvin says. 'I need the money.'

"'I know you do. So quit with this cold feet talk, will ya? I've had enough of blackmailers and turncoats.'

"'Don't worry about me, Duane,' Calvin says. 'I'm in no position to back out.'

"'I know you're not. We'd both be stupid to let ten big ones float away while we sit on our halves.'

"'I know.'

"'So are we set?'

"'We're set.'

"'What's gonna happen?'

"'You're gonna tell Tresh that you've come to your senses, that you see he deserves a little more money, like say fifty grand, and that you'll have a local guy—me—deliver it. Only thing is, what if he wants it dropped off somewhere instead of me pickin' him up? I mean, is he that stupid, he's gonna let a stranger pick him up in the alley after dark?'

"'Oh, make no mistake,' Duane says, 'he's that stupid. Only thing is, if he wants you to make a drop, just set it up so you drop it somewhere you can stake out. Then you drop him right there.'

"'Uh-huh.'

"'Now are we set? Can I count on this gettin' done without worryin' that you're gonna drop off the face of the earth on me?'

"'I'm going nowhere,' Calvin says. 'I'll get it done. What kind of proof do you want? You gonna wait until the papers cover it a day or two later?'

"'No way! I need pictures, man! He turns up missing, he could be gone for months before I know for sure he won't surface again. You bring me pictures.' "

I sat there shaking my head. There was no longer any doubt that Duane was the burglar, that Frank Tresh had had something to do with the grocery store part of the burglary, that Tresh had been paid, and that now he wanted more money for his silence.

It was no wonder everyone assumed he was innocent. He looked like the nicest family man you'd ever want to meet. Could he have taken that huge risk just for money because of his daughter? That was something I wouldn't have minded finding out.

But we had a bigger, more important job to do. No matter what his motive was, no matter how bad Frank Tresh was, we couldn't stand by and let him get murdered. Even if whatever we did resulted in his getting arrested, it would also result in Duane and Calvin getting caught, and it would keep a murder from taking place.

I told Jimmy all I had learned that day.

"This is bigger than I ever thought it would be," Jimmy said. "I told you I thought it was hot, but I had no idea—"

"I know," I said. "What are we gonna do?"

"Hey," he said, "you're usually the one with the answers and ideas. Don't ask me. I will say this, though: we'd better do what's right and do it quick."

I nodded. "Of course you know that nobody's gonna believe us. No matter who we tell, they're gonna think we're crazy kids with wild imaginations."

"Yeah, but at some point we gotta tell someone, right, Dal?"

"Sure," I said, not too convincingly, because I wasn't convinced that anyone would ever believe us until we knew where this murder was supposed to take place and forced them to go with us to make sure it didn't.

"You still want me to watch Calvin's place for a while?" Jimmy said.

"Yeah, I'd kinda like to know for sure that he lives there, and I wouldn't mind knowing who else comes to see him."

"You know what I wouldn't mind knowing?" Jimmy said. "I wouldn't mind knowing whether we're doing the right thing. This isn't something I used to worry about, but now I do, thanks to you."

I smiled. I knew what he was talking about. Jimmy had become a Christian with a very strong conscience, sometimes stronger than mine. It embarrassed me at times when he asked me if what we were doing was what Christians should be doing. In this case, I knew the right thing was to prevent someone's being murdered—that was easy. But at what point should we have told someone else? I feared we were already well past that place, but there was still the problem of no one believing us. I didn't know that for sure, but I'd had it happen before over much smaller problems. Why would anyone believe this crazy story?

The phone rang.

Jimmy and I stared at each other, then bolted for the door. We rumbled down the stairs, stopping at the bottom to see if it would ring again. If it did, that meant it was a normal call. But it didn't. Jimmy moved to the phone and picked up the receiver.

I stood right next to him, my ear next to his, so I could hear too. I thought I couldn't be shocked anymore, but all of a sudden I was part of the case in a way I never expected. We got in on the conversation after it had already begun. Duane was talking to Calvin.

"All I'm saying is that Tresh is spooked. This kid comes nosin' around the grocery store askin' all kinds of questions. Now what in the world was that?"

"How should I know?" Calvin said. "What'd he want to know?"

"Well, he said he'd read about the case in the newspapers at the library, but why would he be doin' that? You think it's just a coincidence? I mean, why now, why the week before this guy's most important appointment ever?"

"I have no idea. Did he know the kid?"

"He said he's a local. He's seen him in the store lots of times. Doesn't know his name. Comes in there with his buddies sometimes, I guess. They have a ball team or somethin'. Nice kids, never had any trouble with 'em."

"Then what's the big deal? Curious kid. Forget about it."

"That's easy for you to say, Calvin. You don't have a sense for these things. I don't like any wrinkles when we're gettin' close."

"How much experience have you had with this kind of a thing?" Calvin said.

"More than you wanna know."

"No. I want to know."

"How many guys, you mean?"

"Yeah, how many have you taken care of?"

"Plenty."

"How many?"

"Why?"

"I want to know."

"Tresh will be number five."

"You do any of these yourself?"

"You know as well as I do, Calvin, that the guy who has it done is every bit as involved as the guy who handles the job, that is if the guy who has it done can be connected with it somehow."

"Yeah, I know. But I still want to know if you've ever done this yourself."

"Once. That's the only way to reach my level."

"Yeah? And what level have you reached?"

"The level where I don't have to do it. I can pay to have it done."

"Keeps your hands clean, huh?" Calvin said with sarcasm.

"In a manner of speaking. The one I did was a family job, a matter of honor. I don't think I lost my soul over it."

"And if I do this for you, you're still clean?"

"I'd like to think so."

Calvin snorted. "Well, I think I can see what it takes to reach your level."

"What's that?"

"A totally burned out conscience."

"Keep in touch," Duane said, as if he hadn't even heard him. He hung up without saying good-bye.

Jimmy hung up and looked at me, shaking his head. What could either of us say? When the phone rang again, we both jumped. Jimmy put his hand on it, waiting to see if it would ring normally. It didn't. Somebody was calling Calvin, or he was calling them.

Jimmy picked up the receiver.

". . . Grocery Store," we heard.

"Good afternoon," Calvin said. "Mr. Tresh, please."

55

7

The New Set-Up

"One moment, please. I'll see if he's available. May I say
who's calling?"

"It's personal."

"I'm sorry?"

"It's private and personal and urgent."

"One moment."

Jimmy and I couldn't believe it. Calvin was calling Tresh?
We thought Duane was supposed to let Tresh know that he
was going to pay him off and that he would be hearing from an
associate. Then Calvin would call him and set up the appointment. We looked quizzically at each other and waited for Tresh
to come on the line.

"Tresh," he said. "How may I help you?"

"It's how I may help you," Calvin said, sounding tougher
than we'd ever heard him with Duane.

"I'm listening," Tresh said, also sounding colder than he
had with me.

"I have a proposition for you, Mr. Tresh, and I was wondering if we could get together and discuss it."

"I don't have any money to invest, and —"

"I'm not talking about an investment. I'm talking about a way to keep a certain person off your back and earn a tidy income in the process."

There was a long pause, then Tresh said, "If the certain person is the person I'm thinking of, I'm on his back. He's not on mine."

"He might be all over your back if you don't listen to me," Calvin said.

"I'm still listening, but if you have access to him, you might want to let him know that I'm running out of patience and will have to do something soon."

Calvin said, "The fact is, sir, the one you think you're pressuring has had enough, and he's about to tell you that you win and that he'll come through with some more for you."

"That's good news. How much?"

"The amount is irrelevant since you're not really going to get it anyway."

Frank Tresh was silent.

"He's gonna tell you you're getting a bunch, the more the merrier, you know what I mean?"

"No."

"The more he tells you, the more likely it is that you'll take the risk to meet with his associate. Only he's paying the associate to get you off his back. Know what I mean?"

"No. What do you mean?"

"Well, he's not talking about spraining anything. Follow?"

"No."

"He's talking about the big one, pal. You're gonna buy it, if you follow my meaning."

"Quit talking in code, man," Frank Tresh said, clearly angry now. "You're telling me that this person will tell me he's going to take care of me, and then he's going to do me in?"

"You got it, Mr. T., and I didn't even hafta draw ya a picture."

"Who am I talking to?"

"You don't really expect me to tell you that, do you, Mr. Tresh?"

"Well, how do you know so much about this scheme?"

"What does that have to do with it?"

"Well, how's it supposed to go down? What's going to happen?"

"I told you. You're going to get a call from your, shall we say, friend. He'll tell you he's paying you off, just like you want, but that he can't be seen with you. He'll tell you you'll hear from an associate. The associate will call, set up the meeting time and place, and you will meet with him because you need the money."

"What if I don't meet with him?"

"You will. The promised payoff will be at least fifty thousand. You need it, and you know it. It will be worth the risk."

"But you're trying to tell me it's more than a risk."

"Oh, yeah. You buy into this, you're history."

"How do you know this?"

"What difference does that make?"

"I have to know who I'm dealing with so I know whether or not to believe you."

"Mr. Tresh, you're talking to the associate who has been assigned to handle the job."

There was another long pause. "So, why are you telling me this? Why don't you just do it and be done with it?"

"Because I have a proposition for you. I'm being paid to do this, you understand."

"I imagine you are."

"I get my money if I can prove the job has been completed."

"Yeah?"

"Help me prove it, and split my payoff."

"Which is how much?"

"What do you care how much it is, Tresh? You do it just to save your neck."

"How much?"

"Five thousand."

"You're getting five thousand for a job like that? I'm insulted."

"Oh, you thought your hide was worth more than that? Don't flatter yourself."

"The fifty I'm asking for is more like it."

"Yeah, and he'll quickly agree to that to get you off his back, and then he pays me a lot less than that to silence you forever."

"How do I know you won't do something to me anyway?"

"Because if I was going to, I would have followed through on the original plan."

"I never would have fallen for that."

"Yes, you would have. I've seen your daughter. You'd have done anything for fifty grand."

There was a silence so long that Calvin must have wondered if Tresh had hung up on him. I couldn't believe Calvin had lied to him and told him he was getting only half what he really was getting for the job. But then, why should I have expected a greedy creep like Calvin to tell the truth?

"Are you still there, Mr. Tresh?"

"I'm here."

"Cat got your tongue?"

"Did you say you'd seen my daughter?"

"Yes, sir."

"I don't like that very much."

"I didn't think you would."

"Do I detect a threat to my family? Because I will not stand for — "

"Let me tell you something straight, Tresh, and I want you to listen because I am not going to repeat it, and when I'm finished I'll no longer be on the phone. Are you listening?"

"Yes," Tresh managed.

"I'm willin' to take a risk for a decent payoff, but I don't want to do to you what I said I would do, OK? So, your neck is safe if you cooperate with me. If you don't, I may do the job, I may not, but somebody will. You know that."

"What happens to me if I cooperate and then this certain gentleman finds out I'm still around?"

"We'll have so much on him by then, he won't dare get near either of us. I'll put all the evidence in a safe deposit box with special instructions in case anything happens to either of us."

"I'll have to think this over."

"You don't have much time, Tresh. When you get his call, you'll know I'm bein' straight with you."

There was another ring in the background.

"That's another call for me," Tresh said.

"There you go," Calvin said.

"You want me to put you on hold?"

"Sure, and have this call traced? I'll call you back." And Calvin hung up.

I agreed to wait by the phone to see if Tresh called Calvin back. Meanwhile Jimmy would ride over to the old Blakely place and see what he could see. Jimmy hadn't been gone five minutes before the phone rang. I waited to see if it would ring normally. I hoped it wouldn't. It didn't.

It was Duane for Calvin. "All right," he said. "It's all set. I told him he'd be hearing from a friend of mine who's gonna give him fifty thousand big ones. You know what he says? He says make it seventy-five thou and I promise you'll never hear from me again. Is that good or what?"

"What'd you tell 'im?"

"What do you think? I said to give me a few seconds to think it over, and then I ask him if he's serious, if he's tellin' me the truth. He says yes. Don't you love it? He thinks I'll believe him if he promises! So I tell him I'll come up with seventy-five grand and that he'll be hearin' from you. You'd better call him right away."

"Yeah. I'll try to set it up for next weekend."

"Oh, yeah, that's somethin' else. He wants to do it tonight."

"Tonight? And he believes you can come up with the money that fast?"

"Don't forget I don't have to come up with it, Duane. All I need to do is to agree and tell him I have it."

"But isn't he going to be suspicious if you can come up with that much cash that fast?"

"I griped and grumbled and told him he was makin' life miserable for me, but that I would do what I could. I also said if he heard from someone today, that meant that I had come up with the money. He told me if he didn't hear from you today, he was going to the authorities. I acted scared like I really didn't want him to do that and like I was gonna do whatever I had to do to come up with the cash. He reminded me that he knew, just like everybody else did, how much I got from the bank. 'You can come up with it,' he said."

"So, you want me to call him now?"

"Yeah. And put a picture in the drop off place tonight. Call me when I can pick it up. If it convinces me, I'll leave the other halves of the five hundreds in the stump."

"OK, Duane."

"No cold feet?"

"'Course, but I'm ready. To think I'll have ten grand by tomorrow morning."

"Just don't mess it up."

"Don't worry."

"Call me when it's done so I know you'll have a picture for me. You got a camera that gives instant pictures?"

"No."

"You can rent one. Or buy one. You'll have the money soon enough."

"OK."

"Good luck."

"Thanks."

I hung up when they did and almost immediately heard another ring. I picked up the receiver and listened, but I didn't hear anything. I was about to hang up when Mr. Calabresi said, "Hello? J.C.?"

"Oh, uh, hi, Mr. Calabresi. I forgot to say hello. Jimmy's outside for a little while but will be back soon. Should I tell him anything?"

"Just tell him we'll be a little late. I'm taking his mother to the antique mall in Park County. We'll be home after dinner."

He thanked me, and when he hung up, I could hear Calvin talking to Frank Tresh.

8

The Double-cross

"OK," Tresh was saying, "you gotta tell me what the guy said to me, so I know you're for real."

"He said you'd hear from me, and now you're hearin' from me."

"What else?"

"You told him it had to be seventy-five thousand, and it had to be tonight."

"OK, so how do I know I can trust you?"

"You don't. It's a chance you're gonna have to take. If I wanted to do you harm, I would have just done it."

"Why don't you want to?"

"Why *would* I want to? Who wants to have to do that if you can get almost the same money for not doing it?"

"How we gonna pull this off?"

"I need to meet you somewhere where I won't be seen. I don't ever want to be associated with this deal."

"Am I ever going to know your name?"

"I'll tell you the same name I gave to your friend. Calvin."

"OK, Calvin. I need to tell you what I'm gonna do. I'm gonna go through with this and take the money, and then I'll leave you out of the rest of it."

"The rest of what? What do you mean?"

"I mean I'm goin' after him again. I may even try to stick him with tryin' to kill me."

"You gotta keep me out of it."

"I said I would. You don't think I'm grateful? If I can believe you, I'm actually making more money than I hoped, and I'm not getting wiped out."

"How do you figure you're getting more than you asked for? I'm only offering you twenty-five hundred. You're not planning on blackmailing me later, are you?"

"You'll have to trust me, Calvin, just like I'm trustin' you. You gotta figure I'm grateful."

"You should be."

"So you name the place."

I was surprised when Calvin gave Frank Tresh directions to the same stumps where the money drop off had been. They set the meeting for eleven o'clock that night.

"Oh, brother," Calvin said, "there's some kid riding his bike on my property."

"A kid came to see me today," Tresh said. "What's he look like?"

"Kinda short and stocky, dark hair."

"Nah. Not the same kid. He still there?"

"He's leaving."

"I'll see you at eleven."

I could hardly stand waiting for Jimmy to get back. I didn't want to leave the phone, though I knew it was unlikely that any more calls would come before the meeting that night.

As soon as Jimmy rode into the driveway I called to him from the door. "You were seen!"

"I was?"

I told him the whole story.

"So now we tell somebody, right?" he said.

I didn't say anything.

"Dallas! You're not even thinking about us going to stake out that meeting, are you?"

Still I said nothing.

"Dallas! No . . ."

I sat down and motioned for Jimmy to do the same. "Listen," I began.

"Dallas, no."

"Just hear me out."

"Dallas—"

"Listen, no murder is going to take place tonight, right?"

"How do we know that?"

"I told you what Calvin said to Tresh, and you've heard all the plans."

"But Dallas, you're making one big mistake. You're believing a criminal. He has accepted money, or at least he's made a deal to murder someone. Just because he tells the victim he's not going to do it doesn't mean he won't. Maybe that's the only way he could think of talking Tresh into seeing him."

"Maybe, but I don't think so."

"You don't think so? You don't know, but you don't think so, and based on your gut feeling we're going to go watch a meeting where a guy might get murdered. It doesn't make sense, Dallas."

He had a point, but I didn't want to admit it. "I still don't think anybody will believe us yet," I said. "We don't have enough to go on. If I were a parent or a policeman or something, I don't think I'd even believe the phone business."

"But if we told somebody now, they could listen in and see for themselves."

I shook my head. I didn't really disagree. I just wanted to go to the meeting and see what happened. It was probably stupid and certainly dangerous, but I just wanted to. "We can take our bikes and stay out of sight. We know that area better than Tresh does, and we've probably spent more time there than Calvin."

Jimmy sat shaking his head. "I don't like this," he said over and over. And when his parents got home, it was all he

67

could do—I could tell—to keep from telling them. I kept giving him a look that told him it was still our secret.

When we went to bed at ten, I told him, "We'll tell somebody soon enough. But let's see what happens at eleven and then decide who we tell and what we tell them. Fair enough?"

He nodded miserably. "Something tells me I'm gonna regret this. You're gonna regret this, and I'm gonna regret letting you talk me into it."

"Don't blame *me*, Jimmy."

"Well, you've already talked me out of telling anybody. What am I supposed to do?"

"Do what you think is right."

"What I think is right is telling my parents and having them call the police."

"Even if your parents believed you, the police wouldn't. Then we wouldn't have accomplished anything. Who would keep Tresh from getting killed, if you think that's what Calvin wants to do to him? And if these guys do pull off this double-cross of Duane, who's gonna see that all three of them get caught?"

He shrugged, and we waited and listened for the rest of the household to get to sleep so we could sneak out in time to stake out the meeting place. We crept down the back stairway at about ten forty-five and carefully pulled open the creaky barn door to get our bikes. When we got to the meeting place we ditched our bikes in the underbrush and moved out to a clump of trees about ten yards from where we had hidden the last time. That put us in the pitch dark area at the end of the stumps, where we could hear better but not be seen.

Calvin arrived first, and I let out a huge, but silent, sigh of relief when he parked his car right behind one of the trees we had hidden behind the last time. What would he have said or done if he had recognized Jimmy after having seen him at his place while he was on the phone earlier in the day?

Calvin whistled softly to himself and sat on the stump farthest from us, setting a plastic shopping bag on the middle stump. From it he pulled a camera and a box of instant picture film. He loaded the camera and fired off a shot of the stump. The flash in that darkness left spots before my eyes. As the camera whirred and whizzed and delivered the exposed film, I worried that my eye and the side of my face would show up in his picture.

I hoped it would be too dark for him to see anything. He sat there waving it in the air to hurry the developing and drying process. He held it up to the faint star and moonlight and scowled, but I sensed it was because he couldn't see well, rather than because he saw something he didn't want to see.

When a car pulled into the clearing, Calvin put his camera and his bag behind one of the stumps and stepped back away from where he could be seen. A door slammed, and Frank Tresh walked slowly into the clearing near the stumps. He looked nervous as he glanced around.

"Tresh?" Calvin whispered, making Tresh jump.

"Yeah."

Calvin came out and shook his hand.

"Let's get this over with, Calvin," Tresh said. "Did you bring the money?"

"Half of it," Calvin said.

"What do you mean, half?"

"Well, hey, I only got half till I prove you're dead."

"Let me see it."

"Sure."

From his pocket Calvin pulled a short stack of bills.

"What are these?" Tresh demanded. "Half bills?"

"That's right. That's all I got, and that's all you're gonna get until I get paid."

"How do I know you're not gonna stiff me on my half when it's all over?"

"What good are my half bills gonna do me? As long as you've got these halves, you know I can't steal your money."

"But what *are* these?" Tresh asked. "There's only a few bills here." He held them up to the light. "These are five hundred dollar bills, you idiot!"

"Yeah! Five of 'em. Twenty-five hundred, just like we agreed."

"We agreed on twenty-five hundred, but you never said anything about worthless bills!"

"I already explained that," Calvin said. "When I give you the other halves, you can tape them together and—"

"And then I'll have worthless five hundred dollar bills! Worthless! What do you take me for, some kind of a fool? I *work* in currency, man! I know these bills have been out of circulation for more than twenty years!"

Calvin looked stricken. "Are you serious?"

"Don't play dumb with me, Calvin. You were plannin' to stiff me all along!"

"Hey! If I was gonna stiff you, why wouldn't I give you the whole bills? The only reason I gave you halves is because that's all I got. My contact must think they're worth something, or he would have given me the whole bills, too."

"Wait a minute," Tresh said. "Your contact is Duane, right?"

Calvin nodded.

"Duane pulled the jobs, dummy. I turned off the alarm system in the store so he could clean out the safe, then waited until after the cops arrived at the jewelry store before turning it on. Then I know he knocked over the bank, because it was in all the papers the next day. But don't you know what he got there?"

Calvin shook his head.

"Over a million bucks worth of worthless five hundred dollar bills."

Calvin sighed and sat on a stump. "That scoundrel," he said.

"You knew nothing about this?"

70

"I swear. In fact, I'll tell you the whole truth, now that I know what Duane is tryin' to pull. He's payin' me ten grand for this job. I told you five to get a bigger share. I'm sorry."

Tresh snorted. "Listen to you, apologizin' to the guy you're supposed to kill. Well, pal, we're gonna be partners because I'm not lettin' Duane get away with this. Are you?"

"No way."

9

To Tell or Not to Tell?

Jimmy and I looked at each other. Now we knew a murder was going to happen, but it wasn't going to be Frank Tresh; it was going to be this Duane, whoever he was. Now I knew we would have to tell someone. If the two of them were going to pull this job, then all three of them would be at the same place at the same time.

"I'm supposed to call him when I'm done, and then he's gonna come here to pick up the picture and leave the rest of the money."

"How were you going to prove I was dead?"

"I'll show you."

From his plastic shopping bag, which came from Tresh's grocery store, Calvin pulled a Halloween novelty toy that contained fake blood. "I was gonna make it look like I had slit your throat."

Tresh laughed. "Let's do it. Let's give Duane something to look at before he leaves the money and then gets the surprise of his life."

"His life?"

"Well, the surprise of his death, then."

Calvin had Tresh lie back across one of the stumps so his body was in the most awkward, unnatural position they could come up with. His head hung back and down, exposing his neck. Calvin splashed the fake blood all over Tresh's neck. Tresh giggled and said it was cold and tickley.

"Hold still while I shoot the picture," Calvin said. "Wanna make it look really realistic?" he asked.

"Yeah," Tresh managed from his strange angle.

"Keep your eyes open. Just stare straight ahead with your eyes unfocused."

I moved to where I had a good view of the picture Calvin was shooting. As Tresh lay there, flopped over the tree stump as if his throat had been cut, he looked horribly murdered. I knew the photo would fool me. In fact, the real live Tresh lying there like that, eyes open, staring blankly in the distance, almost convinced me.

"Wait till you see this," Calvin said. "Just wait till you see it. I don't think I could have shot a more gruesome picture if I had actually cut you." He stood waving the photo in the air, waiting for it to develop.

"You know," Tresh said, "I wish there was a way to get Duane to bring more money. He's bringing you the other halves of twenty five hundred dollar bills?

Calvin nodded.

"Has he got any good money? Like what he took from the store or the jeweler?"

"I doubt it. That was a long time ago. You think he knows the five hundreds are worthless?"

"Probably. He must have read about it in the paper or something."

"I'm surprised I missed it. I should have known he wouldn't hand over that money so easily."

"You would have earned it."

"Yeah, but ten grand to an inexperienced person?"

Tresh shrugged. "I had become a royal pain to him. Not as much as I will be now, though. That picture ready?"

They squinted at it in the darkness. "Wow!" Tresh said.

"Man!" Calvin said. "I'd buy it. Wouldn't you?"

"You bet. Now what do you do with it?"

"I leave it in a stump as proof. I call Duane. And he comes and gets it and leaves the money."

"What are you supposed to do with my body?"

"Take it and dump it somewhere. He doesn't care where. That's my problem."

"We'd better make this look like a murder scene. You got any more of the fake blood? Splash it around the base of the stump and then drag me on the ground and sprinkle it after me, like you dragged me to the car."

"What are we going to do with Duane?" Calvin said as they set up the scene.

"It's got to be quick and clean," Tresh said. "One of us is going to have to drive his car with his body in the trunk and dump it somewhere."

"How about if I pick you up at the store, and we hide my car in the underbrush here?" Calvin said.

"OK, but what are we going to do to Duane? We're going to share the job, right?"

"The only way I know to do it is to club him, put him in the trunk of his own car, and drive his car maybe down the ravine at the quarry."

"Sounds good. How will we jump him?"

"He'll be least suspicious of me," Calvin said. "I'll come up on him when he gets to the stump, and I'll talk to him about wanting more money."

"What if he's got a gun?" Tresh asked.

"I never thought of that."

"Think of it."

"Maybe I'd better have one, too."

"Do you have one?"

"No."

"Then how are you gonna get one before dawn?"

"I guess I'm not. Do you have one?"

"Nope. But I have a toy gun that looks real. If you can scare him, get the drop on him before he reaches for his, I can sneak up behind him and knock him out. I'm willing to do that, but you're going to have to do the rest."

"What do you mean, the rest?"

"You're going to have to finish him."

"I don't know about that," Calvin said. "What if your beating him over the head finishes him?"

"It won't. I won't hit him that hard."

"Well, I don't want to stand there and hit him some more. If he's out, we can drag him to the car, then run the car down into the quarry, like I said."

"And you think that will do it?"

"Sure. I'll go home and call him and tell him it's done and that the picture is in the stump. Then we'll have to get right back out here and wait for him."

"Yeah, what if he beats us out here?"

"We just can't let that happen."

Calvin placed the photo in a stump, and they hurried to their cars.

Jimmy turned to me. "This is it, Dallas. We've got to tell everything we know, and fast."

I agreed, and we hopped on our bikes. I had no idea how difficult our task would be.

When we got to Jimmy's the lights were on both in his bedroom and his parents' bedroom. "Uh-oh," he said. "They'll be calling your parents before long."

I ditched my bike in the front yard and raced to the door where I jabbed at the bell. I heard Mrs. Calabresi call to her husband, and he came pounding down the stairs. He swung the door open and gasped. "Dallas! What are you doing out there? Where's James?"

"Right here," Jimmy said.

"Get in here," his father said. "You have a lot of explaining to do."

76

"It's my fault, and I *can* explain," I said, as Mrs. Calabresi came downstairs and we all sat in the living room.

"How did you know we were gone?" Jimmy asked.

"I don't know what that has to do with your being gone after dark without permission, but if you must know, we got a wrong number."

"You did?" I said, panting. "What was it? What did they say?"

"It was a wrong number, Dallas," Mrs. Calabresi said, clearly annoyed with me. "I told you."

"But it was one man talking to the other," I said, "an older man and a younger man, and the younger told him the job was done and the photo was finished, something like that?"

"That's just what you told me, honey," Mr. Calabresi said, his face pale. "What is going on here? How did you know that?"

"You're not going to believe this," Jimmy said.

"Try us," his mother said. "I want to know what's going on, and I want to know right now."

Jimmy began the story with the first phone call he'd heard, and because his parents had heard a couple of them themselves, they believed us. They were not happy, however, about our not telling them before. "That was about the stupidest thing you could have done, both of you," Mr. Calabresi said.

"I didn't think anyone would believe us," I said.

"We wouldn't have been able to afford not to, Dallas."

"Sir, all due respect, if you're going to call the police, I think you ought to do it now. Is Duane heading over to the pickup spot to see the photo and drop off the money?"

Mr. Calabresi nodded and went to the phone. That's when I noticed that Mrs. Calabresi was crying. "When I think," she said, "how dangerous that was—" She burst into sobs.

"I'm sorry, Mom," Jimmy said, and he gave me a look I hope I never see again. I couldn't argue with the fact that this was my fault. I had badgered him into investigating this crazy scheme with me and not telling anyone, and now he was taking the heat. Of course, I would be getting mine soon enough.

Mr. Calabresi hurried back into the room. "OK, boys, the detective, Sergeant Manning, will be here in a few minutes. I'm going to get dressed. He wants to pick us up so you can show him exactly where this meeting place is. Then you have to stay out of the way. I'll tell you, I'm glad you finally came to us, but I'm going to have to deal with you for not coming to me sooner."

I didn't know what that meant for Jimmy, but I knew for me it meant that my parents would hear about it. Mrs. Calabresi said she knew that if she were in my mother's position, she would want to know. "Even in the middle of the night," she said as she headed for the phone. "I'm sure your parents are going to want to wait here with me until you get back."

"Actually, you'd better go there. They can't both leave my sisters."

"Good thought," she said, and she suggested it to my mother. I heard Mrs. Calabresi talking softly and quickly in soothing tones to my mother, assuring her that we were OK and that we would be fine, even though we were going with the police to the scene of a crime. "I'll be over in a few minutes," she told her, "and we'll wait together. . . . Talk to Dallas? I really don't think there's time just now. My husband is on his way out the door with the boys. They'll be fine. I'll be right over."

I dreaded facing my parents after this night was over.

We skipped out the door and down the steps and into an unmarked squad car carrying a stocky detective in his fifties. "My partner's on his way," he said, after introducing himself. "Tell me where we're going so I can tell him by radio."

We did and as he raced down the road he asked us to run over the whole story for him again, too.

"Calvin," he said. "That has to be Calvin Herr from Indianapolis. We knew he had moved into the Blakely place, but we thought he was keeping his nose clean. We knew Duane Decker was a safe cracker and that he's been in the area, but we never could pin any of those three jobs on him. We even knew he liked to pull multiple jobs on the same night, but there was nothing to get hold of until now. This is beautiful, especially if you boys are willing to testify in court."

10

The Chase

We got a one-minute lecture from Detective Manning on the way, too. By the time we got near the spot, I was convinced that we should have told the police early. They knew these guys, had tried to connect Duane with the crimes, and the detective even suspected Tresh all along ("though we never had enough to go on").

As we pointed out the clearing where the stumps were, Detective Manning relayed the information over his radio. He reminded the other police officers to come with their lights and sirens off, and in unmarked cars. He sent cars to stake out Tresh's, Herr's, and Decker's homes while the rest were to surround the meeting place.

"But sir," I said, "we're going to be lucky to get there in time."

"You may be right," he said. "But I don't have any choice."

"You'd better park here, behind these trees," I said. "Calvin will probably park in back of that parking lot down there, because he won't want Duane to see him and Tresh."

"Thanks," Detective Manning said simply, and he wheeled the big sedan in behind the trees.

"They're already here," Jimmy said quietly, causing Detective Manning to whirl around in his seat and look at him.

"What? Where?"

Jimmy nodded and pointed toward some bushes on the other side of the clearing near the stumps. "I saw something shiny reflecting out of there," he said.

We all peered out into the darkness. Sure enough, something was there.

"Show me where the stumps are," the detective said. Mr. Calabresi, Jimmy, and I all reached for our door handles at the same time. "Whoa, wait a minute," Manning said. "Only one of you should be with me just now. Who's it going to be?"

"Me," I said, just as Jimmy and his father were saying, "Dallas."

"That makes it unanimous," Manning said. "Let's go, son."

I slid out and bent low as the detective was doing as we hurried into the underbrush. "Take me the long way around," he whispered.

"OK," I said, "but how do we stay away from Tresh and Calvin? They're trying to do the same thing we're doing."

"Their car is on the far side, away from where Duane will be to see it. My guess is they'll stay close to it. If we do this right we can circle around behind them before Duane gets here. Now point at the stumps."

"I can't see them from here."

"I know, but you know where they are. Point to where they should be."

I made my best guess as we kept moving, and I pointed through the underbrush.

Manning looked at me. "Every time I look at you, no matter where we are, you point to where you think the stumps are. We'll find out what kind of a detective you'd make."

As we crept through the woods, between bushes, and over clumps, I watched for the detective's face to turn toward me in the moonlight. When it did, I pointed. We were making a large circle around the outside of the area. Manning put a finger to his lips, looked at me, saw me point toward the stumps, and then himself pointed into a dark area. I looked. There was Calvin's car. Or at least I thought it was Calvin's car.

"You know whose car that is?" he said so quietly I could hardly hear. I shook my head. "Tresh's. They must have brought only one car."

"How did Calvin get here then?"

"Either Tresh picked him up, or—"

Suddenly Manning dropped to his knees and pulled me down into the leaves. He put his hand over my mouth, and we heard a bike approach and someone lean it against a tree.

Calvin crept past within twenty feet of us. "Tresh?" he whispered.

"Yo," Tresh responded. "Shh . . ."

Calvin moved to join Tresh and then hid behind trees looking out onto the stump area.

"Don't reply to this transmission until I get my earpiece in," Manning whispered into a walkie-talkie he had pulled from his pocket. "Two-eighteen, I need to know your ten-twenty. I'll tell you when I'm ready to receive." He turned to me as he wrestled with the tiny earphone. "I asked my partner for his location," he said. "He's the one who will stick with Decker if anything goes wrong. He's assigning someone to—"

Just then, before he could plug in the earphone, his partner answered his request. "We're next to your car, two-twenty," came the loud, staticky words from the radio.

Manning swore and fell on the walkie-talkie, muffling any further transmission. Tresh came hurtling past Calvin and jumped into his car. Manning mashed a finger on the talk button and growled into the radio, "You just blew our cover, Ernie! They're on the run in a four-door Chevy just south of you. I'm on foot, and I don't want to spook Decker. He doesn't know they're here anyway, so let 'em get out a ways before you take 'em."

"Sorry, Sarge," came the reply.

Manning stuffed the walkie-talkie into his coat pocket and reached into a shoulder holster for his pistol. "Stay put," he said. I was happy to. As Calvin raced for the car, a club in his hand, Manning chased him. Tresh started the engine and backed up, reaching over to open the passenger door. Calvin was diving in when Manning flew through the air, his massive body blind-siding Calvin and knocking him rolling in the dirt. The club wound up under the car.

Tresh gunned the engine, throwing grass and dirt and pine needles into the air, and the door slammed as he sped off, charging through unpaved areas and out on to the frontage road, tires squealing. I heard the powerful squad car engines light out after him.

Manning grunted and groaned as he struggled to his feet, unable to see Calvin in the darkness. The smaller, younger man leap-frogged the detective and ran to his bike. As he started to climb aboard, Manning caught his sweatsuit from behind. Calvin picked up the bike and swung it, knocking the big man down again.

I knew Manning had the gun, but I also knew he didn't want to make a noise so loud that it would scare off Duane Decker, who should arrive any minute.

Calvin set the bike down and ran along beside it before mounting. He had trouble keeping his balance and gaining momentum pedaling over the rough ground and thick grass, and as he came past me I saw Manning limping after him. "Oh, don't do this to me," Manning said. "I'm old." Into his walkie-talkie he panted, "Following bicyclist Herr on foot. May lose him. More important not to spook Decker. We know where Herr lives."

As I watched, terrified, I could see that Manning was not gaining on Calvin. And what would happen if he got into the clearing and Decker happened to drive up? He wasn't expecting anyone, not even Calvin, certainly not Tresh, and least of all the police. The other officers had no idea where we were

84

and would have caused too much commotion charging in to find us.

I didn't have time to think how foolish I was being, but I was sure Calvin had no weapon. I took off after him, quickly catching up to Manning.

"No!" the detective shouted. "You gotta stay outa this!"

"I can catch him!" I said.

"No! Don't!"

But Manning was still limping, and as I flew past him I was gaining on Calvin. Just before he got past a row of trees, I drew even with his back tire and kicked his axle. I wasn't able to knock him over, but I did make him wobble and slow down. That gave me time to find a stick about a foot long and a couple of inches thick. I grabbed it and started after him again. I could hear Manning wheezing behind me, now cheering me on

"Knock him down, and I'll take him," he rasped.

I drew even with Calvin's bike again, just as he reached the frontage road. I hoped a squad car or two would appear over the rise, but they didn't. Two were heading the other way after Tresh. I dove toward the back tire with my stick and drove it into the spokes as I scraped along the pavement, knowing I had damaged my elbows and knees.

The sound of metal against metal made me think that Calvin was about to go down, but in the faint light I saw him wobbling down the road. I had apparently damaged his ten-speed gear apparatus, but he still had enough spokes and gears to keep moving. He pedaled off down the frontage road as I struggled to my feet.

Manning lumbered out from the woods. "I've got to get back to the clearing to see if Decker shows up," he said. "You go straight back to the car."

"I know where he's going," I insisted.

"So do we," Manning said. "We know where he lives. Now back to the car."

Manning turned and pushed his way back toward the stumps. I looked both ways on the frontage road and saw Calvin pedaling one way and nothing coming the other. If they knew where he lived, why didn't they go after him? I knew he would want to get to his car. I didn't know what I was going to do, but I couldn't let him do that.

I began running. I ran toward the corner where I could see his place. He had turned left and was going, of course, the long way. Rather than following him down the road, I cut diagonally across the fields. The running was rough over cold, dried furrows, but I knew his bike was slow too and that he had a lot farther to ride than I had to run.

I knew I would be winded. I knew I would have chest pains that wouldn't quit, but I had to keep going. I ran as fast as I could, trying to think of what to do to stall him so he couldn't get away.

About half way there I turned to see where he was, and he was in the middle of the street, off the bike, looking both ways, trying to fix something. I kept running. He was back on the bike, laboring along. I would beat him by maybe a minute. What could I do in a minute?

I thought about tearing out his phone line, but I hoped the police knew enough about the story by now that they would be waiting by the Calabresis' phone. If he tried to make any frantic calls for help, they would know his every move. What else might he try?

If I were in his place, I would think I had a better chance to escape by car. I might go in the house for a weapon first, or even a change of clothes or some food if I thought I was going to be on the road for a long time. But then I would be heading for that car.

I would have just seconds to locate the car. If he kept it where the Blakelys had kept theirs, it would be in a shed directly behind the house. The important thing now was to keep him from seeing me. Whatever I was going to do to his car, I was going to have to do fast.

Could I pour sand or dirt in the gas tank? How long would that take to reach the engine? Could I let air out of one of his tires? No, that would take too long. Could I puncture a tire? I doubted I was strong enough, even if I could find a knife. Could I unplug something in the engine? Probably, but I didn't know enough about car engines to know what to pull.

I was out of breath, my heart crashing. I had a big lead on Calvin, but I didn't know if I could hang on. "Lord, help me," I prayed. "I want to do something right for a change. I know I was wrong in not telling anyone, but now I want to help. Let me help. Let me make it in time to do something right. And protect me, please."

11

The Arrests

Lucky for me the main light over Calvin's shed was off, but there was one of those darkness-triggered lights on his barn at the side. I was able to get into the shed without being seen, and then, from a little of that light shining through the cracks in the side walls, I could see his car.

I felt inside and found his keys in the ignition. I knew he would have another set, but I wanted to slow him down, so I pulled the keys out and tossed them into a corner of the garage.

Then I reached under the dash and pulled the hood release lever. The hood popped, but it took me several seconds to figure out how to get it all the way open. Then I couldn't see well enough to know what to try to mess up so I slammed the hood and opened the gas tank. I scooped dirt from the floor into the tank, not knowing quite what that would do.

I started letting the air out of one of the front tires, but it was taking too long. I felt around on Calvin's workbench for something sharp and found some old ice tongs. I hacked away at one of his tires but couldn't tell if I was doing any damage. I heard him in the driveway. He tossed his bike aside and burst through the back door of his house. I saw him rummaging around inside, grabbing clothes from the bedroom and stuff from the kitchen. I also saw him pull a shotgun down from a rack on the wall. I wanted to get out of there, but so far I wasn't sure I had done anything to slow his escape except for what I put in his gas tank.

I scrambled under the car and wedged one side of the ice tongs under his rear wheel so when he backed up it would puncture the tire. I peeked out. He was still in the kitchen. The only thing I could think of was to get back under the hood of the car and jam something into his radiator fan. I knew that would cause some problem, but I wasn't sure what.

But car tires are thick and strong, and I worried that if he was able to run over the ice tongs without hurting his tire, he might be able to drive several miles before the dirt in the gas tank gave him any trouble. I whipped open the driver's side door and popped the hood release again. Before I tried to open the hood all the way, I grabbed the first hard things I felt on the workbench, a huge screw driver and a monkey wrench. I heard the house door slam. I wouldn't have time to get under the hood.

Through a crack in the wall next to the door of the shed I could see Calvin running toward the car. As he pulled the big wood doors noisily open, I shuffled under the tool bench and out of sight. I hoped against hope he wouldn't notice that the hood had been released and was up about an inch. He slid into the car and reached for the ignition key. I heard him swear and smash his hand on the dash. He jumped out of the car and ran back into the house.

Did I have time to stick the screw driver and the wrench into the fan? Probably not, but I had to try. I listened to see if any squad cars were heading our way. There was no sound on the street. This time I didn't have any trouble getting the hood open. I stuffed the screwdriver near the fan and felt what I thought was the fan belt give a little. I wondered if it would do any good to yank that belt out of the grooves. I dug into it with the screwdriver and felt it fall loose. Then I took the wrench and forced it between the fan blades and the radiator. With the belt loose and the blades jammed, at least something was messed up.

I looked around the car to see where Calvin was and saw him swing open the back door of the house. How could I shut the hood without him hearing it? Maybe I could get it down just far enough to catch without slamming, and he wouldn't notice. But it was heavy. What if I got it started and it wouldn't stop? I had to time it so it would slam just when the back door did. But what if I was early, or late? I prayed.

He came through the door. I started the hood down. It crashed in my ears. I hadn't heard the house door before the hood hit, and I didn't hear it after. "Thank you, Lord." But what if he hadn't shut it yet? I peeked. The door was shut. And here he came.

And there I stood at the front of the car in the dark. I didn't have time to get under the workbench. I crouched by the front bumper. In the distance I heard a car roar onto the street to the north of Calvin's place. I didn't know if he could hear from inside the car, but he had to know the police would be on his trail soon.

When he started the engine, the racket under the hood was unbelievable. It sounded as if the whole car was about to fall apart. The belt I had loosened had not been the fan belt but probably the air conditioning belt or some other, and so the fan was trying to work against that wrench.

Calvin hesitated, almost as if he was going to get out and check under the hood, but he changed his mind and threw the car into reverse. It rose up on one side as the rear tire began to roll over the ice tongs. When it was right above them and all its weight bore down upon them, the tong punctured the rubber and it exploded and hissed. Calvin jerked around in his seat, giving me a chance to dive back under the workbench.

When Calvin looked back he must have seen the red lights of a squad car reflecting off his house because he just kept going, backing out in spite of the racket under the hood and his flat back tire. The car was hard to control, and as he tried to turn around and head out of the driveway his car swerved all over the place. The squad car was turning onto his road now, only about a quarter mile away. Calvin pushed the accelerator to the floor and the good rear tire bit into the gravel and dirt and screamed out onto the road. He was fighting against the bad tire that was pulling the car the other way. Calvin turned right to try to outrun the squad car, but when he got about a mile down the road he must have thought better of it with his clanging engine and flapping tire. Another squad car came toward him from the other direction.

He tried to turn around in the street and almost went down into the ditch before he finally had the car facing the other direction, heading toward the squad car that had now stopped in front of his house near the center of the road to block Calvin from getting past. There was just enough room on either side for him to squeeze by, so the officer was waiting for Calvin to commit himself one way or the other before getting in front of him.

By now the rubber on the flat tire had rubbed so much against the body of the car that it had begun to smoke. Calvin gunned the engine and moved to the right of the squad car, and that flat tire burst into flames. The police car moved left just a little to get in front of him, but Calvin had lost control. His car slid down into the ditch and almost rolled over. It flopped back down as the officers from both cars jumped out with guns drawn.

I wondered if Calvin would come out of that car with his shotgun blazing, but he didn't. He leaped out with his hands over his head, and while a policeman stood with his microphone in his hand, warning Calvin over his loudspeaker to stay still, Calvin whined, "I didn't do nothin'! I didn't get no real money, and I didn't kill nobody anyway! I never stole nothin'! I never broke no laws! I'm innocent!"

No one had seen me. My job was done. I ran back across the fields almost as fast as I had come. Had Duane Decker arrived, or had all the commotion scared him off? My legs were wobbly and my knees watery as I headed straight for the stumps. A hulking, dark figure crouched at the edge of the clearing and turned on me, pointing a gun at me as I approached. I froze.

It was Manning. "Get down," he whispered. "And don't move."

"He's not here yet?"

"Just arrived," Manning whispered, nodding toward Decker's car, idling in the parking area. "I wouldn't have believed it, but somehow we kept from scaring him off."

We heard him making his way cautiously through the weeds and into the clearing. He checked all three stumps before finding the photograph. He held it under a small flashlight and chuckled.

"All right!" he said. He sat on the stump and studied it. "All right!"

"Now!" Manning shouted, scaring me half to death. From three different spots around the area circling the stumps came blinding lights from hand-held police spotlights. "Hands on your head, Decker!"

Duane was a middle-aged man with dark hair and a thick overcoat. He jumped as if he'd been shot, and when he reached inside his coat, a half dozen cops moved in, shouting, guns aimed at his head. "Drop it or you're a dead man, Decker!"

He raised his hands over his head, the picture floating to the ground. One of the officers picked it up and looked at it in the light. "You'd better not have had anything to do with this, Duane," one said.

"Don't worry about that," Manning said. "This was a phony murder. The victim was just picked up north of here, and the hit man was picked up a mile away."

"What?" Decker said. "It didn't go down?"

"Nope. You're under arrest for conspiracy to commit murder and for burglary. You have the right to remain silent. If you waive that right, anything you say can be used against you in a court of law. If you cannot afford an attorney, one will be provided for you. Do you understand these rights as I have explained them to you?"

"Yeah."

Decker was handcuffed and led away.

"I'll take you home, hero," Manning said. "Where've you been?"

I told him what had happened when he had told me to go back to the car. I could tell he was fighting a smile. "That was pretty foolish, and pretty dangerous, but the report we got said Calvin was a pretty easy arrest because his car seemed to be falling apart. I confess I wondered if you hadn't had something to do with it, after I saw what you did to his bike."

"I was trying to put my stick in his front spokes," I said. "Then he would have gone right over the top."

"Yeah, and then even an old, fat, out-of-shape cop like me could have caught him."

When we got back to the car Jimmy and Mr. Calabresi were still waiting for us. "We heard a lot of activity on the radio," Mr. Calabresi said. "Sounds like everyone has been apprehended."

"That's right," Detective Manning said. "We got them all, thanks to you boys."

"Sounds like it got kinda hairy," Jimmy said. "Calvin and Tresh almost got away?"

"Not really," Manning said. "They weren't gonna get far with all the manpower we had and all the information we got from you and your friend here."

"You could do us a favor," Mr. Calabresi said. "You could have somebody call the O'Neils and tell them we're on our way and that everybody's safe and sound."

"Happy to," Manning said, and while he was radioing headquarters to request that call, Jimmy sat back and sighed.

"Funny thing was," he said, "after all that, after how involved we were from the beginning, we both had to just sit back and watch at the end. I mean, except for you showing De-